First Candlewick Press edition in this form 2003

Library of Congress Catalog Card Number 2002101339

ISBN 0-7636-1969-8

2 4 6 8 10 9 7 5 3 1

Printed in Hong Kong

This book was typeset in Kabel Book Alt.
The illustrations were done in watercolor and ink.

Candlewick Press
2067 Massachusetts Avenue
Cambridge, Massachusetts 02140

visit us at www.candlewick.com

Bunny Love

Two Stories by Anita Jeram

Bunny My Honey
All Together Now

CANDLEWICK PRESS
CAMBRIDGE, MASSACHUSETTS

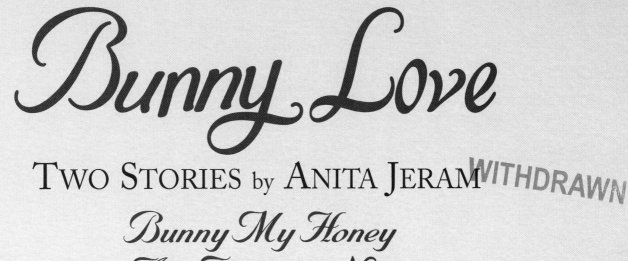

Bunny My Honey

$\mathcal{M}$ommy Rabbit had a baby.
His name was Bunny.
He looked just like his mommy,
only smaller.

He had long ears, a twitchy nose,
and great big feet.
"Bunny, my Honey,"
Mommy Rabbit liked to call him.

Mommy Rabbit showed Bunny how to
do special rabbity things,

like running and hopping,

digging and twitching his nose,

and thumping his great big feet.

Sometimes Bunny played with his best friends,
Little Duckling and Miss Mouse.
They played quack-quacky games,
squeaky games, and thump-thump-thumpy games.

They sang, We're the little Honeys.
A little Honey is sweet.
Quack quack, squeak squeak,
Thump your great big feet!

If a game ever ended in tears,
as games sometimes do,
Mommy Rabbit made it better.

"Don't cry, my little Honeys,"
Mommy Rabbit said, "I'm right here."

But one day Bunny got lost.

Oh, how could such a bad thing happen?

Perhaps it was a game that went wrong.

Perhaps Bunny ran too far on his own.

But there he was, just one lost Bunny.
The more Bunny looked for his
friends and his mommy
the more lost
and the more lost
and the more lost
he became.

Bunny started to cry.

"Mommy, Mommy,

I want my mommy!

Mommy, Mommy,

I want my mommy!"

"Bunny, my Honey!"

What was that?

"Bunny, my Honey!

Bunny, my Honey!"

"Bunny, my Honey!"

"MOMMY!"

Mommy Rabbit picked Bunny
up and cuddled him.
She stroked his long ears.
She put her twitchy nose
on his twitchy nose.
She kissed his great big feet.
Bunny's ears and nose
and feet felt warm all over.

"I love you, Mommy,"
Bunny whispered.
"I love you, Bunny, my Honey,"
Bunny's mommy
whispered back,
"and I love my other
little Honeys, too."

On the way home, Bunny and
Miss Mouse and Little Duckling
sang their song.

We're the little Honeys.
A little Honey is sweet.
Quack quack, squeak squeak,
Thump your great big feet!

And Bunny was a
happy rabbit.

All Together Now

When Mommy Rabbit says,
"All together now,"
one thing Bunny, Little Duckling,
and Miss Mouse often do is sing
their special little Honeys song.

"All together now!" …

We're the little Honeys.
A little Honey is sweet.
Quack quack, squeak squeak,
Thump your great big feet!

In the little Honeys song,
"A little Honey is sweet" is Bunny's special line.

Bunny was Mommy Rabbit's first little honey,
before Little Duckling and Miss Mouse came along.

He was always as sweet as can be.
That's why Mommy Rabbit called him
"Bunny, my Honey."

In the little Honeys song, "Quack quack"
is Little Duckling's special line.
Its special meaning is,
I'm yellow and fluffy and
good at splashing and sploshing.

It means, even if I don't look like a bunny,
Mommy Rabbit's still my mommy just the same.

When he was born,
Little Duckling came from an egg.
The first surprise was when he hatched.
Bunny was just peeping at the egg
when it cracked open and out
came Little Duckling.

The next surprise was when
Little Duckling followed Bunny home
and became his brother and
the second little Honey.

In the little Honeys song, "Squeak squeak"
is Miss Mouse's special line.
Its special meaning is,
I've got a pink itchy-twitchy nose
and a pink squirly-whirly tail.

It means, even if I don't look like a bunny,
Mommy Rabbit's still my mommy just the same.

Miss Mouse first arrived when Bunny
and Little Duckling found her all alone in the
long grass early one summer morning.
Miss Mouse wasn't frightened.
She just seemed to need some
love and affection.

Mommy Rabbit soon made
her one of the family,
a new sister and a third little Honey.

As well as singing their special song,
the little Honeys play all sorts
of special games together.

They play splashy-sploshy games,
which Little Duckling is best at.
They play itchy-twitchy, squirly-whirly games,
which Miss Mouse is best at.

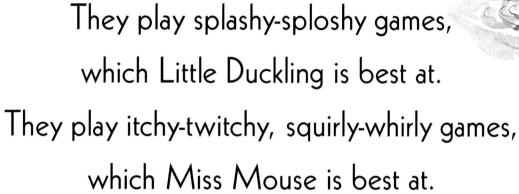

They play run-rabbit-run games,

which Bunny is best at.

Best of all, they play the
Thump-Your-Great-Big-Feet game,
which they are all best at together
because they all have

Great Big Feet.

Bunny has
Great Big Feet.

Little Duckling has
Great **Big** Feet.

Miss Mouse has
Great **Big** Feet.

And sometimes
Mommy Rabbit
plays with them,

which is extra-specially special

because Mommy Rabbit has the

Greatest,

Biggest

Feet of all!

The Thump-Your-Great-Big-Feet game goes like this:

thump!

thump!

thump!

thump!

thump!

We're the little Honeys.
A little Honey is sweet.
Quack quack, squeak squeak,
Thump Your Great Big Feet!